The Adventures of
TAXI DOG

The Adventures of
TAXI DOG

by Debra and Sal Barracca
pictures by Mark Buehner

▪▪▪▪▪▪▪▪▪▪▪▪▪▪▪▪▪

PUFFIN BOOKS

PUFFIN BOOKS
Published by the Penguin Group
Penguin Putnam Books for Young Readers, 345 Hudson Street, New York, New York 10014, U.S.A.
Penguin Books Ltd, 27 Wrights Lane, London W8 5TZ, England
Penguin Books Australia Ltd, Ringwood, Victoria, Australia
Penguin Books Canada Ltd, 10 Alcorn Avenue, Toronto, Ontario, Canada M4V 3B2
Penguin Books (N.Z.) Ltd, 182-190 Wairau Road, Auckland 10, New Zealand

Penguin Books Ltd, Registered Offices: Harmondsworth, Middlesex, England

First published in the United States of America by Dial Books for Young Readers, a division of Penguin Books USA Inc., 1990
Published by Puffin Books, a member of Penguin Putnam Books for Young Readers, 2000

3 5 7 9 10 8 6 4 2

Text copyright © Debra and Sal Barracca, 1990
Illustrations copyright © Mark Buehner, 1990
All rights reserved

THE LIBRARY OF CONGRESS HAS CATALOGED THE DIAL EDITION AS FOLLOWS:
Barracca, Debra. The adventures of Taxi Dog/by Debra and Sal Barracca;
pictures by Mark Buehner.
p.   cm.
Summary: A stray dog in New York City is adopted by a taxi driver, with whom he thereafter rides and shares adventures each day.
ISBN 0-8037-0671-5. ISBN 0-8037-0672-3 [lib. bdg.]
[1. Dogs—Fiction. 2. Taxicabs—Fiction. 3. New York (N.Y.)—Fiction. 4. City and town life—Fiction. 5. Stories in rhyme.]
I. Barracca, Sal. II. Buehner, Mark, ill. III. Title.
PZ8.3.B25263Ad 1990 [E]—dc19 89-1056 CIP AC

Puffin Books ISBN 0-14-056665-1

Printed in Hong Kong

*For all the homeless and abused creatures of the world—
may they all find peace some day.*
D.B. and S.B.

To Mom and Dad
M.B.

My name is Maxi,
    I ride in a taxi
        Around New York City all day.
I sit next to Jim,
    (I belong to him),
        But it wasn't always this way.

I grew up in the city,
    All dirty and gritty,
        Looking for food after dark.
I roamed all around,
    Avoiding the pound,
        And lived on my own in the park.

One day a car stopped—
    Its tire had popped.
        Out stepped a tall man, I could see.
He came over and said
    As he patted my head,
        "Are you lost? You can come home with me!"

Did I hear right? Oh, boy!
My tail wagged with joy—
I jumped right up on the seat!
He said, "My name's Jim,"
I could ride home with him
And he'd give me some good food to eat.

I ate and I ate,
I cleaned the whole plate.
Then Jim took a scarf of bright red.
He tied it around me,
So glad that he found me,
And kissed me on top of my head.

My wish had come true—
I would start life anew.
At last I had a warm home
With someone to love me
And take good care of me—
No longer would I have to roam.

Jim said, "Your name's Maxi,
You'll ride in my taxi,
We'll ride all over the town.
We'll see all the sights,
All the streets and the lights,
We'll go riding uptown and down."

There's so much to see!
    Every building and tree
        With people and cars everywhere.
All the interesting places—
    New friends and new faces
        Each time we pick up a fare.

One time a big lady
    Who said she was Sadie
        Was singing that night in a show.
She broke into a song
    And I sang right along—
        You couldn't tell me from the pro!

"To the hospital, quick!
   My wife is quite sick,"
      Cried a man as we stopped for the light,
"Our baby is due!"
   And like lightning we flew—
      We made it in time—what a night!

Sometimes when it's slow
　　To the airport we go.
　　　　We get in the line at the stand
To wait for a fare,
　　And a hotdog we share
　　　　While we watch the planes take off and land.

The door opened wide—
    Guess who jumped inside?
        Two clowns and a chimp they called Murray!
"We're performing at eight
    And our flight came in late—
        To the circus, and please try to hurry!"

We get such big tips
   On most of our trips—
      Jim is surprised at this treat.
But he doesn't know
   That I put on a show
      For the passengers in the backseat!

At the end of each day
    When we've earned our pay,
        We drive the cab back to its spot,
Where our boss named Lou
    Says, "Hi! How'd ya do?
        Have a biscuit!" (He likes me a lot.)

It's just like a dream,
   Me and Jim—we're a team!
      I'm always there at his side.
We never stand still,
   Every day's a new thrill—
      Come join us next time for a ride!

ABOUT THE AUTHORS

Debra and Sal Barracca work with many artists and writers of children's books
through their young company, Halcyon Books.
Both are native New Yorkers and they were inspired to write
The Adventures of Taxi Dog after riding in a taxi whose owner kept his dog
with him in the front seat. They will donate a portion of the book's
proceeds to The Fund for Animals in New York City.
The Barraccas live in Croton-on-Hudson, New York with their three cats.

ABOUT THE ARTIST

Mark Buehner grew up in Utah and graduated from Utah State University.
Mr. Buehner works as a freelance illustrator and
The Adventures of Taxi Dog is his first book. He now lives with
his wife and two children in Brooklyn, New York.